Written by **ABHISHEK TALWAR**

Illustrated by **SONAL GOYAL**

The Adventures of
BIPLOB THE BUMBLEBEE

VOLUME 1

PUFFIN BOOKS
An imprint of Penguin Random House

PUFFIN BOOKS

USA | Canada | UK | Ireland | Australia
New Zealand | India | South Africa | China

Puffin Books is part of the Penguin Random House group of companies
whose addresses can be found at global.penguinrandomhouse.com

Published by Penguin Random House India Pvt. Ltd
7th Floor, Infinity Tower C, DLF Cyber City,
Gurgaon 122 002, Haryana, India

Penguin
Random House
India

First published in Puffin Books by Penguin Random House India 2019

Text copyright © Abhishek Talwar 2019
Illustrations copyright © Sonal Goyal 2019

10 9 8 7 6 5 4 3 2 1

ISBN 9780143446996

Typeset in Sabon LT Pro
Book design and layout by Akangksha Sarmah
Printed at Replika Press Pvt. Ltd, India

www.penguin.co.in

Dedicated to my loving
wife, Ritika, for always believing.
And to my curious children, for
inspiring these tales.

A special thank you to Preeti
and the team at FunOkPlease.

1
FLYING POLLEN

So much to do, so little time to do it in, thought Biplob as he reached the garden and set about getting ready to start his day.

Biplob buzzed around the garden saying hello to all his friends. 'Good morning, Ms Sunflower. I hope you're doing well today,' he said to one.

'Hello, Ms Gladiolus. I hope you got enough water this morning and aren't thirsty like you were yesterday!' he wished another.

In return, all his friends waved their stalks and smiled at Biplob.

This is going to be a fine day to collect nectar and store it in my nest for the winter. I'd better start working without wasting a single minute, thought Biplob as he buzzed to a sunflower.

Biplob worked tirelessly, flitting from flower to flower and collecting nectar.

All of a sudden, he overheard two squirrels talking to each other. 'Look at that selfish bee. All he does is suck nectar from the poor flowers all day long,' said one squirrel to the other.

'Yes,' replied the other squirrel, 'he has no consideration for their feelings. Look at us. We only pick acorns that have already fallen on the ground. We don't harm the trees.'

Biplob was taken aback.

Ms Gladiolus, who was about
to give Biplob some nectar,
was surprised.

'What is the matter, Biplob?
Why have you stopped collecting
nectar from us? And why are you
crying, my friend? Tell us, please.
Maybe we can help you.'

Biplob hung his head in shame. 'I have been so selfish. I keep taking nectar from all my wonderful friends, but I do nothing in return! I wish I was able to do something for you!'

On hearing this, all the flowers burst out laughing.

'Oh, you silly bee!' exclaimed Ms Sunflower. 'Bees are our best friends.
It is only thanks to you that this garden is so full of flowers.'

'Yes, sir!' added Ms Hibiscus. 'If it weren't for you,
we would have withered away a long time ago.'

'But how am I responsible for you not withering away?' sniffled Biplob, looking surprised.

'You don't realize how much you do for us, Biplob!' piped up all the flowers together.

'All flowers have something powdery called pollen. For a new plant to be born, this pollen has to be transferred from one plant to another. But plants can't walk around.

'So, each time a bee sits on us to take nectar, our pollen gets stuck to its legs. Then, when the bee sits on another flower, this pollen is dropped off there. Before you know it, a new plant is born because of pollination.'

'Oh, I was just happy to carry pollen from one flower to another since you are all my friends,' replied Biplob. 'I never knew that it helps to grow more flowers and plants!'

Biplob somersaulted in the air. He buzzed all over the garden again, collecting nectar to his heart's content and transferring pollen as he always had. All the flowers laughed at the happy bee's antics.

Life was back to normal in Biplob's garden.

2
BIPLOB THE WATER FARMER

It was another lovely rainy day in Biplob's garden. He was lying lazily on his tummy, looking at the water droplets. *How fresh and clean everything looks in the rain!* he thought.

Biplob's friends, the flowering plants, were also happy
with the rain. After all, more rain meant more water for them.

As Biplob enjoyed the view, he said aloud, 'I hope it rains for long so that
Farmer Balram's well fills up with enough water to last until next year's monsoons.'
He then flew out to see how far the water level had risen in the well.

As Biplob reached the well, he found Farmer Balram
standing there with a frown on his face. 'What are you thinking about?' asked Biplob.

'I'm just thinking, Biplob. It's raining so heavily this monsoon. But my well has such a small mouth.
A whole lot of water is just flowing away and going to waste, instead of being collected. I'm afraid
once the rains stop, we may not have enough water for the summer,' said Farmer Balram.

Biplob looked down and realized that Farmer Balram was right. Most of the rainwater had collected in little puddles on the ground and then formed small rivulets that flowed into the fields and on to the road. 'Oh, that's such a shame! Barely a trickle is making its way into the well, if at all!' exclaimed a worried Biplob.

The next morning, Biplob was still lost in thought about the well. *How can we save this water from flowing away? If only I could do something to help the rain flow into the well instead of it washing away,* he wondered.

Just then, Biplob looked up to see water gushing out from a drainpipe on Farmer Balram's roof.

Excited, Biplob raced to Farmer Balram and asked him, 'Why don't we harvest the rainwater and use it during the dry months, just as you harvest your crops?'

'Don't trouble me, Biplob. How on earth can you harvest water? I've never heard of anything so strange before,' said the annoyed farmer.

'You *can* harvest rainwater, Farmer Balram. Look there!
Do you see the water rushing out from the pipe along the wall of your house?
The water that gets collected on your roof flows down through this pipe!
Let's connect this pipe to your well. This way, the water goes straight into it,' said Biplob.

'You just may have something there, Biplob. If this works, I can create little ducts and guide the rainwater into the well!' said Farmer Balram, excitement rising in his voice.

'What is a duct, Farmer Balram?' asked Biplob.

'Simple. We dig little pathways or channels all around the well to help the rainwater find its way in.' Farmer Balram started building the ducts with gusto. He also connected the drainpipe from the roof to the well, and the two immediately saw the results of their hard work.

'What a wonderful idea, Biplob!' Farmer Balram clapped his hands with joy. 'We are not only harvesting rainwater but also saving it.'

'We can use this water in the fields and garden for a long time now,' said Biplob with a smile. 'The flowers will never go thirsty again!'

3
BIPLOB SAVES THE DAY

'Time to spruce up for the big day, ladies,' exclaimed Biplob as he circled the garden. 'I just heard Farmer Balram say that the district flower show is on the 4th of next month!'

'I'm sure we will win all the prizes,' said Ms Gladiolus, swaying merrily in the breeze. 'I don't think the gladioli have ever looked this good, all thanks to a careful diet of sunshine, water and manure.'

That night, all the flowers and Biplob dreamt of winning the flower show.

CALENDAR

4

DISTRICT FLOWER SHOW

When Farmer Balram and Biplob went into the garden the next morning, they were in for the shock of their lives. The young plants looked weak and dull—their leaves were shrivelled and their drooping stems almost touched the ground!

'What's happened to all the new plants?' asked Biplob.

The older flowering plants cried loudly,
'We don't know! They were perfectly
fine when we went to sleep last night.'

'This seems to be some sort of insect attack,' said Farmer Balram grimly. 'We need to spray the strongest pesticide to teach these bugs a lesson.'

'But the flower show rules state that we can't participate if we use pesticides!' Biplob reminded him.

'What else can we do? I would rather have my plants live than be eaten by pests, even if it means not participating,' replied Farmer Balram. His mind was made up. He left to buy pesticide, saying he would return in the evening.

PESTICIDE

Biplob thought hard about this problem. There had to be a way to save the young ones without breaking the rules of the show.

Just then, he saw Ms Violet perk up and say, 'Aphids! Aphids are the problem.'

'Huh? What are those?' said Biplob, frowning.

'When I was a young plant in the nursery, a kind ladybug called Carla
used to take care of us. She spent all her time crawling over our leaves
and stems. But she never spent any time with the older plants.

One day I asked her, "You're such a warm and friendly creature,
Carla. So why do you ignore the older plants?"

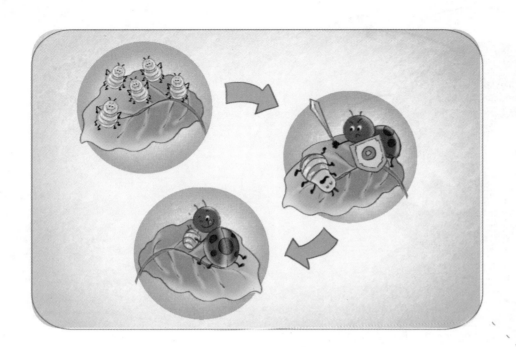

'Her answer took us all by surprise. When Carla was with us, she was actually keeping us safe from aphids. These are insects that eat the leaves and stems of younger plants. They can ruin an entire plant in very little time,' explained Ms Violet.

'Oh! Tell me where I can find this friend of yours and I will bring her here in a jiffy to help us,' promised Biplob.

Ms Violet gave him the address, and he flew away as fast as his little wings could take him.

After flying for two hours, he finally reached the nursery. It was the most amazing sight—there were thousands of young plants with hundreds of ladybugs crawling over them!

Biplob asked around for Ms Carla and eventually found her among the roses. He introduced himself and explained the problem to her. But his heart broke when she said she was sadly too old to travel with him to his faraway garden.

Biplob's wings drooped with worry.
Ms Carla had never seen a bumblebee look so sad.
An idea came to her. She smiled and quickly gathered twenty of her best ladybugs.

'There is a new challenge that only you, my brave and hardworking boys and girls, can tackle,' she announced. All the ladybugs puffed up with pride. 'My old friend Violet's garden has been attacked by aphids, who are killing her poor baby plants. I need you to save them!' Looking at Biplob, she continued, 'Biplob here will take you to Violet's garden, which will be your new home. Remember to put your training to good use and say hello to Violet for me.'

In no time at all, Biplob was back in the garden with the army of ladybugs.
All the newcomers immediately got to work, clearing the aphids from the young plants.

'Quite a mess we have here!' said one between mouthfuls.

'Yes, pity we weren't here earlier,' replied another.

'Well, this is home now, so let's stop
chattering and put our house in order,'
scolded a third.

When a tired-looking Farmer Balram came back to the garden, lugging his spray can and bottles of pesticide, Biplob buzzed happily and reported, 'We won't be needing that any more!' He explained everything that had happened.

'I wish I'd thought of this,' said Farmer Balram. 'We wouldn't have faced this problem at all.'

'Better late than never, Farmer Balram,' replied Biplob happily.
'The young plants will be healthy and free of aphids very soon!'

'Thank you, Biplob and Ms Violet, for finding the perfect natural solution,'
said everyone in unison.

Once again, Biplob the bumblebee had saved the day with his inventive thinking.
He went to bed and dreamt of medals, now that everything was all right in his beloved
garden. No matter what cropped up next, Biplob would be able to find a solution!

About the Author

Abhishek Talwar is a Mumbai-based entrepreneur. He runs a marketing firm and is the founder of Beanstring, India's first social-rewards platform. The stories in this book were created by Abhishek for his children, Aditya and Avantika, to entertain and educate them while having loads of fun!

About the Illustrator

Sonal Goyal completed her masters in fine arts from College of Art, Delhi, after which she worked as the creative head at a leading publishing house for ten years. She is now an independent artist. Her love for drawing and books has led to her drawing *for* books. She spreads smiles by creating cute and lovable illustrations.